IBSN: 978-0-578-79042-8

Written by: Coy Christmas & William Christmas

Cover by: Steve Worthington

Interior design by: Natalie Peterson

Illustrations by: Steve Worthington, Natalie Peterson, Ken Salinas, and Adrian Golden

Production by: HIYAA LLC

Website: www.that2020book.com

FIRST EDITION

All Materials used, Designed, Illustrated, and Manufactured in the great United States of America

2020 unmasked

Table of Contents

If you give the Dems your rifles,
they'll probably want your Glocks.

They'll want to take your guns
from the barrels to the stocks.

It will start out so innocent,
they'll scream "AR-15!"

"Those fully automatic rifles
are just way too mean."

"Why does a gun need 30 rounds?
Why do you need such power?"

"Just dial in 911,
they'll be there in about an hour."

But once you make these small concessions, they'll start to grow bolder.

"I think the Second Amendment applies to only 1800s or older."

Soon ATF is in your house,
your 12-gauge has to go.

They'll take the Sig, 9, and Colt
with nothing left to show.

But you can keep your hunting gear.
"Hunting's fine," they'll say.

Until they come back next month
to take those guns away.

Now you're left with nothing much:
a baseball bat and knife.

"You believe your property is worth
more than a life?"

You watch as thieves break in and steal,
and you can only stare.

They have the guns you wish you had;
of laws they do not care.

The Dems left you defenseless,
even cooking is a chore.

Make sure to grab a knife license
when you go by the store.

As more and more laws begin to change,
you think of fighting back.

But they took all the guns you see,
before you could attack.

You'll think, "Wait I'm American!"
You'll scream, "I know my rights!"

But just the thought of protesting
is jail time for 3 nights.

Now Dems want to control your speech,
they want to change the 1st.

"We have a list of acceptable words,
but opinions are the worst."

"If it doesn't fit our guidelines,
then you have nothing to say."

"We do not want to hear your thoughts,
and do not start to pray."

ACCEPTABLE

UNACCEPTABLE

"How did it ever get this bad?
Who would've thought", you'll say...

But if you give the Dems your guns,
they'll take your rights away.

In our story, there are three
small business owners.

The time had come for them to seek
their fortunes, and build their first stores.

The first small business owner built his restaurant with no defensive measures because it was the easiest thing to do.

The second small business owner built his store with a security system so the police would come help.

The third small business owner built her store with iron bars to ensure that no one could get in.

One night during a protest, the big bad looters, who dearly loved to steal from local small business owners, came along and saw the first small business owner in his defenseless restaurant.

They said "Let me in, let me in, small business owner, or I'll huff and I'll puff and I'll break my way in!"

But without any defenses, the looters huffed and they puffed and broke right in, beat up the business owner, and took what they wanted.

The looters then came to the store with a security system.

"Let me in, let me in, small business owner
or I'll huff and I'll puff and I'll break my way in!"

"Not by the hair of my chinny chin chin," said the second business owner.

The second business owner secretly pushed the security alarm button in relief.

But the looters huffed and they puffed and broke into the store within minutes.

They beat up the business owner
and took everything they wanted...

...and left before the police could get there in time to stop the crime!

The looters then came to
the store with iron bars.

"Let me in, let me in, small business owner, or I'll huff and I'll puff till I break my way in!"

"Not by the hair of my chinny chin chin," said the third business owner.

Well, the looters huffed and they puffed, but they could not break into the store with iron bars.

The looters would not give up, and they left to grab a battering ram to make a way into the store.

The third business owner saw the looters coming back with their battering ram and went to get her gun.

The looters finally returned to try again.

They saw that the third business owner was armed and prepared.

Not only was she prepared, but the first and second small businessmen had shown up to help defend her store!

That was the end of her troubles with the big bad looters as they were cowardly looters and would not fight an armed and prepared small business man...or woman.

The Little Red Entrepreneur

Illustrated by Nat Peterson

There once was a little red entrepreneur with big dreams. She was friends with a lazy unemployed, a liberal politician, and a noisy socialist.

One day, the little red
entrepreneur had an idea.
She would start a business.

"Not I," mumbled the lazy unemployed.

"Not I," said the liberal politician.

"Not I," yelled the noisy socialist.

"Then I will," said the little red entrepreneur. So, the little red entrepreneur designed the product all by herself.

When she finished designing the product, the little red entrepreneur asked her friends, "Who will help me market the product?"

"Not I," mumbled the lazy unemployed.

"Not I," said the liberal politician.

"Not I," yelled the noisy socialist.

"Then I will," said the little red entrepreneur. So, the little red entrepreneur marketed the product all by herself.

When she finished the marketing campaign, the little red entrepreneur asked her friends, "Who will help me take the product to the public to sell it?"

"Then I will," said the little red entrepreneur.

So, the little red entrepreneur took the product to the public all by herself, turned the product into revenue, and took the revenue back to the business.

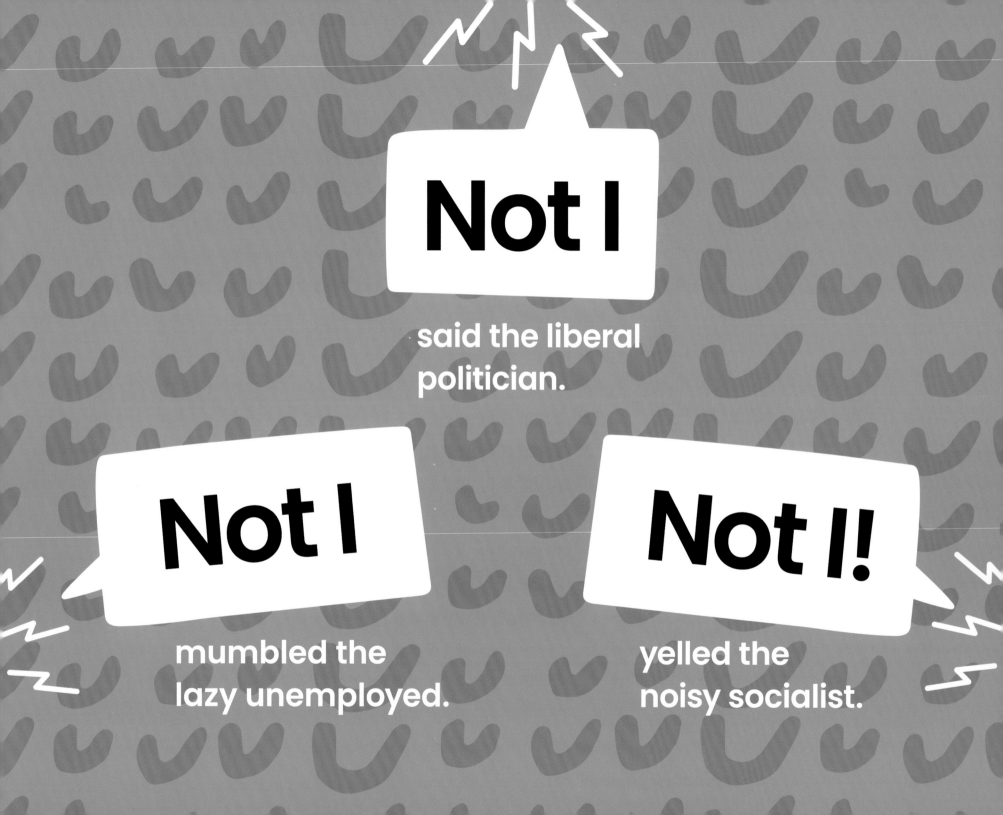

"Then I will," said the little red entrepreneur. So, the little red entrepreneur expanded the business all by herself.

When the expansion was finished, the tired little red entrepreneur looked around at her profits.

The lazy unemployed, liberal politician, and noisy socialist talked amongst themselves and asked, "Who deserves some of the profits?"

"Not you!" said the little red entrepreneur.
"I do." And the little red entrepreneur
reflected on her hard work and the
benefits that would come from it...

I will give back to our economy by giving good benefits to all of my employees.

I will pay off my debts, then plan a vacation to contribute to the world's economy.

I will go shopping and support fellow business friends.

The Little Orange Engine that Made America Great Again

Illustrated by
Adrian Golden

Chug, chug, chug. Puff, puff, puff. The Little Train ran along the tracks. She was a happy Little Train. Her cars were full of good things for the people in America. There were all kinds of tax cuts. Tax cuts that helped the hard-working American to make sure their money stayed theirs. There were domestic manufacturing incentives. Bringing work back to American soil and boosting the economy. There were improved relations with the Middle East. Relations grown from peace treaties and diplomatic advancements.

The Little Train carried all sorts of things that Americans would want. The Little Train was taking all these good things over a mountain to get to America. "How happy they will be to see me!" said the Little Train. But all at once the train came to a stop. Her wheels did not move at all. Her engine did not chug. "Oh, dear," said the Little Train. " What can be the matter?"

She tried to start up again. She tried and tried, but her wheels just would not turn. The Little Train did not know what to do. Just then a shiny new engine came puffing down another track. "Maybe that engine can help me! She began to wave a red flag. The Shiny New Engine slowed down. The Little Train called out to him. "My engine is not working," she said. Will you pull my train over the mountain?"

The Shiny New Engine was not friendly. "You want me to pull you?" he asked. "That is not what I do. I only do politicians' bidding. They sit in cars with soft seats. They look out the windows. They eat in a nice dining car. They even sleep in a fine sleeping car. Me, pull the likes of you? I should say not!" And off went the Shiny New Engine without another word.

How sad the Little Engine felt! Then she exclaimed, "Here comes another engine. A big, strong one. Maybe this engine will help me!" Again, the train waved her flag. The Big Strong Engine came to a stop. The Little Train called out, "Please help me, Big Strong Engine. My engine is not working, but you are big and strong, will you pull me over the mountain?"

But the Big Strong Engine did not want to help. "I do not have time to pull you," he said. "I pull cars full of heavy government spending. I pull big budgets and expensive contracts. I have no time for the likes of you." And away puffed the Big Strong Engine without another word.

By this time, the little train was no longer happy. Suddenly, she saw in the distance another train coming by. "Oh, another train is coming! A little orange engine pulling no cars. Maybe this engine will help me." The Little Orange Engine saw the train waving her red flag and stopped at once.

"What is the matter?" he asked. "Oh, Little Orange Engine," cried the train. "Will you pull me over the mountain? My engine is not working. If you do not help, I cannot get these good things to the people. "Please, please help me."

"Oh my," said the Little Orange Engine. "I am just one small engine. I have not done something like this before."

"But we must get there in order to make America great again," said the Little Train. "Will you try?"

The Little Orange Engine thought about the people on the other side of the mountain and how much they would benefit from what this little train was carrying. The Little Orange Engine pulled up close and took hold of the discouraged, broken train. A hopeful smile crossed her face. At last the Little Orange Engine said, "Make America great again, great again, great again."

Then, the Little Orange Engine began to pull. He tugged and he pulled. He pulled and he tugged. Puff, puff. Chug, chug went the Little Engine. "Make America great again, great again, great again." Slowly, slowly, the train started to move. Puff, puff. Chug, chug. Toward the mountain went the Little Orange Engine and his companion. All the time he kept saying, "Make America great again, great again, great again." As they passed through a dense forest, echoes of impeachment and scandal rang out! The Little Orange Engine just kept saying "Make America great again, great again, great again."

In the distance the brave engine saw the mountain range nearing and knew that they would soon be at their destination! Coming around a bend they were stopped by a herd of sheep that were grazing on the trash left from the passengers on the Shiny New Engine.

Once the sheep cleared his path to chase after the Shiny New Engine, the Little Orange Engine started pulling the Little Train and her cargo toward the town. As they approached the mountain range, they had to change tracks to navigate the obstacles from the Pandemic. The determined orange hero kept saying "Make America great again, great again, great again." Up, up, up. The Little Orange Engine climbed and climbed. At last he reached the top of the mountain.

Down below lay the city. "Hurray! Hurray!" cried the Little Train in tow.

"Thank you! The people will be so happy. All because you helped us, Little Orange Engine."

The Little Orange Engine simply smiled. As he puffed down the mountain, The Little Orange Engine seemed to say… "I knew I could, I knew I could, I knew I could, I knew I could."

That day the townspeople took the good things delivered to them and

began making improvements to their town. They were able to support

small business, pay off debts and grow their defenses.

All thanks to the
Little Orange Engine
that Made America
Great Again!

'Twas the night after Election

Illustrated by: Ken R. Salinas

'Twas the Night After Election, when all through
the House,

all the Democrats were running and scheming about;

Their ruses at play had started to work,
so they sat back and watched, all with a smirk.
They started with mail-ins to vote one time more.
Why not vote in 3 states to help even the score?

They had such high hopes and numerous plans,

with visions of laws and rules and bans,

Now let's bring in loved ones though long in the grave:
Aunt Susie, poor Kevin and Great-Uncle Dave
would surely have voted the way I would vote.

And let's get the pets, the cat and the goat,
a stray down the street; they should all have a say
to ensure we win on this election day.

With the swing states gone red, we've more work to do

Burst a pipe down in Fulton, to make it go blue.

Call Arizona early before the night's done.
No need to keep counting, we've already won.

Now mail-ins are tricky, let's all go to sleep.
When we awake there will be a big leap
in votes for the left, but none for the right.
PA and MI will be such a sight.

As they cheered with their glasses, they talked further
plans
with visions of laws and rules and bans.

Oh, the fun they will have, when they will have won.
They'll fill up their pockets while the work isn't done.

They'll preach about unity, but then they'll divide.
"We're in this together, if you're on our side."

Create bigger government, each branch they'll expand;
they'll have such control over all of the land.

Let's have some more riots, defund the police.
Ensure that the violence will not ever cease.

"We can't let our plans be changed in the least.
Government must have control from the West to the East
so that we can sit here and have all the power."
They laughed as they conspired for the next hour.
But as they sat plotting, they were not aware
That he heard it all, he knew the affair.

Trump won't stand for this fraud, to court he will go
to make sure the votes were counted just so.
There will be exposure of all of their tricks,
so the election process can finally be fixed.

So we mustn't lose hope, there is much we can do.

Vote for local officials that know what is true.

Be involved in your city, stand up for what's right.

Happy Election Day to all, and to all a good night.

To the Reader

WOW! 2020 has been quite a strange year. I keep seeing on social media that in the future it's a year of history to be removed and never spoken of. We can't have that! The left has gone too far with their overall desire to remove one of the greatest Presidents we have ever had, President Donald J. Trump!

These short stories were written as a way for me to put my emotions from pen to pad versus whining about them on social media, blocking streets or rioting. There are productive ways to get your message out and there are ones that make no sense!

The United States of America is the greatest country in the world. We have the bravest men and women protecting our freedom every day. They deserve our respect!

As Americans we should be able to work hard, and our hard work dividends pay off for us and our families; not given to someone that doesn't want to put forth the effort. We are created equal from birth; we all can be the best if we put our minds to it. President Trump wants the USA to be "Great Again", and I will help him.

This book was thought of in the USA, designed in the USA, the material used to make the book is from the USA, it was manufactured here in the USA, the money made from the book will be spent here in the USA and the taxes generated from it will better the USA. 100% ALL USA!!!!

God Bless the USA, God Bless Trump and God Bless all of you!

To my Family & Friends

I would like to thank my wife and kids for being supportive of my hard work. I would like to thank all of my family members and friends that have protected our freedom by serving in the military. I would like to thank my closest friends for being there late at night when I needed someone to talk to.

I would like to give a super big thank you to my brother, William Christmas, for being the co-Author to these stories. Will, you are the man and lyrical genius!

The political opinions of these stories are not necessarily the same political opinions of the illustrators. The illustrators did the work so they can make money to feed their families during this strange 2020. I would like to thank them very much for taking on the job and doing fantastic work!